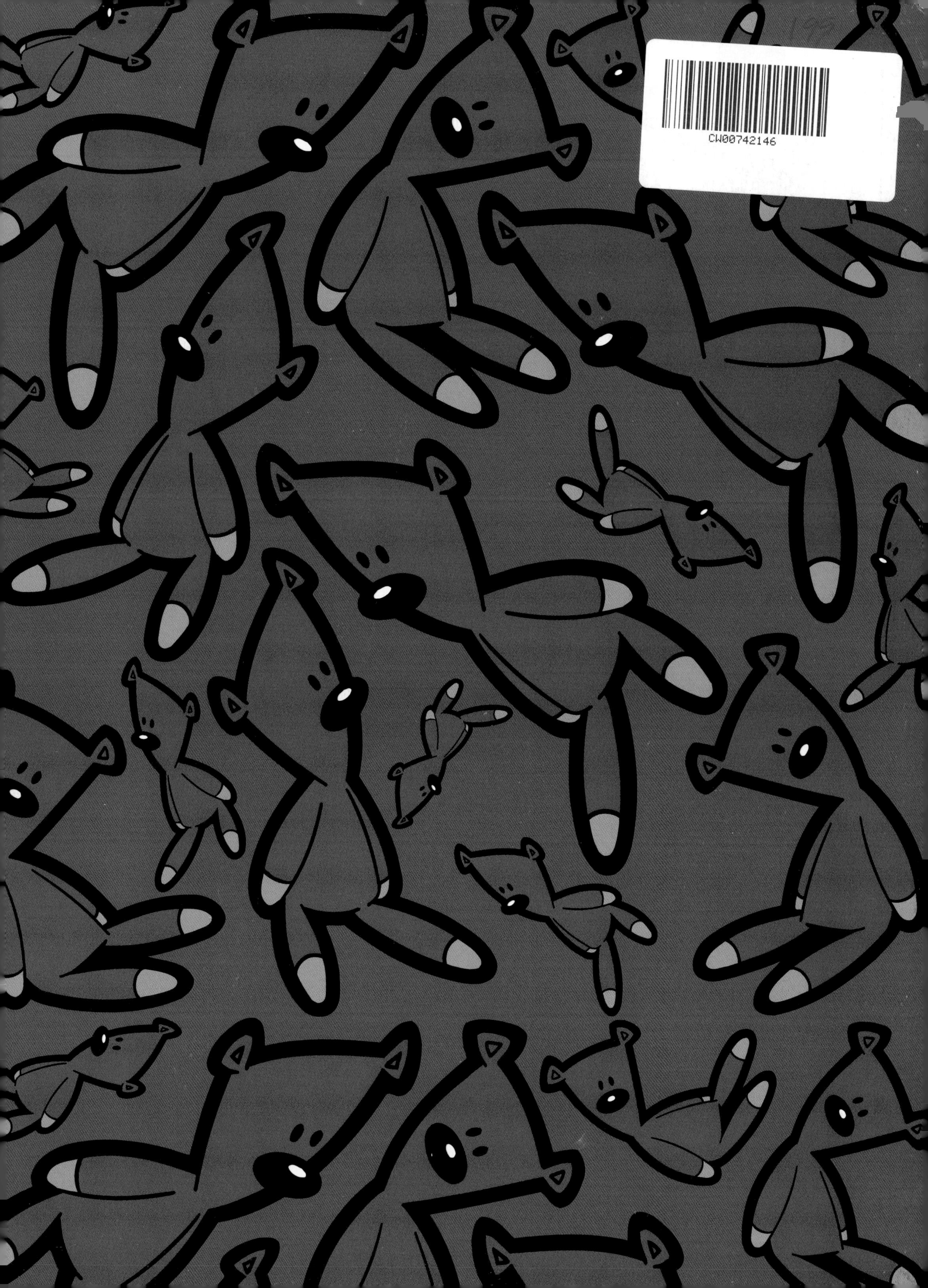

MRS WICKET

IRMA GOBB

Published by Carlton Books Ltd 2002

20 Mortimer Street
London WIT 3JW

SCRAPPER

ISBN 1 84222 632 0

A CIP catalogue for this book is available from the British Library.

Project Manager: Rod Green
Art Director: Diane Spender
Design: Dave Jones
Additional artworks: Red Giraffe
Production: Janette Burgin

MINI

THREE WHEELER

Mr Bean ANNUAL 2003

CARLTON BOOKS

FACTFILE

NAME	Mr Bean
ADDRESS	c/o Mrs Wicket "Daffodils" 12 Arbor Road London N10
LIKES	Teddy, fudge, chocolate, cake, chocolate fudge cake, a nice cup of tea, photography, my Mini, watching telly, white water rafting and helicopter bunjee jumping (last two untried)
DISLIKES	Scrapper, golf, smoking, bottom disturbances (see 'Favourite Food'), nosey parkers, noisey parkers, nasty parkas and that bloke down the park with a wart on his nose, little blue three-wheeled cars
FAVOURITE COLOUR	Green for Minis, red for ties
FAVOURITE FOOD	Beans (see 'Dislikes')
BEST BOOK	Collecting Stuffed Toys by Ted E. Bear Mini Maintenance Manual by Hans D. Spanner
BEST MOVIE	Gone With The Wind (see 'Favourite Food' and 'Dislikes')
PERSON MOST LIKE TO MEET	Whoever it was that let their dog poop on the pavement beside my Mini. I have a little present for him

NAME	Teddy Bean
ADDRESS	c/o Mr Bean (who helped me write this) c/o Mrs Wicket "Daffodils" 12 Arbor Road London N10
LIKES	Mr Bean, staring at the telly, staring at people, staring at the ceiling, staring at the walls, staring generally
DISLIKES	Blinking and being sucked up inside the hoover
FAVOURITE COLOUR	All bear colours – brown, black, white, grizzly and koala
FAVOURITE FOOD	Only eat live crocodiles. Have been on diet for some time
BEST BOOK	The Stupid Bears Who Ate Porridge by Goldilocks
BEST MOVIE	Paddington versus Godzilla (not yet made but it's only a matter of time)
PERSON MOST LIKE TO MEET	Rupert

NAME	Mrs Wicket
ADDRESS	"Daffodils" 12 Arbor Road London N10
LIKES	Peace and quiet, rent day
DISLIKES	That nutter upstairs who never pays his rent on time
FAVOURITE COLOUR	The colour of rent money
FAVOURITE FOOD	Tea and biscuits
BEST BOOK	The rent book
BEST MOVIE	A Fistful Of Dollars
PERSON MOST LIKE TO MEET	Bean on rent days

FACTFILE

NAME	Irma Gobb
ADDRESS	Flat 16a 84 Splendid Crescent London N10
LIKES	Reading romantic novels with my teddy Lottie, travelling to exotic places, nice clean buses, flowery wallpaper with matching curtains, skirts and hats, cute furry animals (but not mice), lavender, comfy shoes, chocolate (but not chocolate mice)
DISLIKES	Mr Bean's driving, noisy eaters, rude people, custard, rude people eating custard noisily, smelly feet, the word 'gargoyle', gargling (sounds too much like gargoyling and is noisy and rude), mice
FAVOURITE COLOUR	Pastel pink and lilac
FAVOURITE FOOD	Jam sponge
BEST BOOK	Eating With Your Mouth Closed by Ella Fatricky
BEST MOVIE	Bambi
PERSON MOST LIKE TO MEET	Prince William, Prince Charming, or any handsome prince, really

NAME	Mini
ADDRESS	c/o The Street Outside Mrs Wicket's "Daffodils" 12 Arbor Road London N10
LIKES	Mr Bean, a nice drop of oil, a full petrol tank, being cleaned and polished
DISLIKES	Rude Mercedes, road hogs, door slammers, cheap spanners and that little kid from down the road who shoved a potato up my exhaust pipe
FAVOURITE COLOUR	Green
FAVOURITE FOOD	Unleaded
BEST BOOK	My Two Lovely Minis by Ivan Uvverwun
BEST MOVIE	The Italian Job (where Minis show loads of other cars how to drive)
PERSON MOST LIKE TO MEET	Chitty Chitty Bang Bang and Fab 1

I wrote this!
signed Mr Bean

And I wrote this!
Hee-Hee!
signed Mrs Wicket

NAME	Scrapper
ADDRESS	c/o Mrs Wicket's armchair "Daffodils" 12 Arbor Road London N10
LIKES	Mrs Wicket, mice, fish, chasing insects, attacking that loony Bean
DISLIKES	That loony Bean, getting wet, anyone standing on my tail
FAVOURITE COLOUR	Any mouse, fish or insect colour
FAVOURITE FOOD	See 'Favourite Colour' and 'Likes'
BEST BOOK	Tiger In My Bed by Claude Buttocks
BEST MOVIE	The Lion King
PERSON MOST LIKE TO MEET	Bean when he's least expecting me!!

THE BOTTLE

Mr Bean was bored. He looked across at Teddy, sitting in his usual seat in front of the television. Teddy looked bored, too. He beamed at Teddy and suggested a trip out in the Mini. Teddy just carried on looking bored.

Mr Bean sighed and wandered over to the goldfish bowl. He gazed in at the goldfish, bored. The goldfish gazed back out at him, bored.

Mr Bean thought about it for a second and came to the conclusion that being a goldfish was probably a good deal more boring than anything else in the whole world. It was probably more boring than being stuck in a stinky traffic jam for four hours on a wet Wednesday in Wolverhampton when the radio is stuck on the same boring station and the last sucky sweet has just popped out of your mouth and got all fluffy on the floor. That had happened to him once. The goldfish couldn't even go out for a spin in the Mini. Mr Bean could though, and he decided to do just that.

Twenty minutes later, he had parked the Mini in the centre of town and was glancing in the window of a rather strange antique shop.

Most of the things on display looked fairly dusty, old and horrible, but one thing caught his eye – a ship-in-a-bottle! Fantastic! He had always been amazed at how they

managed to fit an enormous model of a sailing ship, with masts and sails, through the skinny neck of a bottle. He dashed inside the shop and the door slammed shut behind him.

Moments later, he dashed back out again, the gleaming glass bottle cradled in his hands, and the door slammed shut behind him again. It slammed shut so quickly that it hit Mr Bean in the bottom and he stumbled forward, off balance, jiggling the fragile bottle from hand to hand like a jittery juggler with spiders in his pants. He tripped on the kerb and jiggled even more, then a car roared past and he juggled frantically. He couldn't relax until he had his precious ship-in-a-bottle safely strapped in to the passenger seat of his Mini and was on his way home.

Mr Bean couldn't wait to show the ship-in-a-bottle to Teddy. He fumbled for his keys at the front door and the ship-in-a-bottle clinked against the empty milk bottles on the doorstep as Mr Bean set it down while he searched his pockets. As soon as he had the door open, Mr Bean snatched up his bottle and bounded up the stairs to his flat two at a time. He found Teddy sitting in his armchair staring at the television. He slipped in between Teddy and the telly with his hands behind his back and dared Teddy to guess what he was holding. Teddy just stared straight ahead. Undaunted, Mr Bean produced with a flourish . . . an empty milk bottle! He'd grabbed the wrong bottle downstairs!

Just then, Mr Bean heard the unmistakable clinking of milk bottles and the even more unmistakable whine of the motor in the milkman's float. He bounded over to the window just in time to see his ship-in-a-bottle disappearing on the back of the milk float, stacked in a crate alongside all of the empties.

He thundered downstairs and gave chase in the Mini, even pulling alongside at one point and reaching out to grab the ship-in-a-bottle while steering with his feet. It was only the thought of getting caught up in some traffic lights in the middle of the road and being stretched between the Mini and the milk float until he was 72 feet tall that made him duck back inside the car.

By the time he'd caught up with the milk float again, it had two others for company. The three milk floats headed in through the gates of the local dairy and the gates clanged shut behind them.

The entire dairy compound was surrounded by a high wall. Trying to sneak a peek inside, Mr Bean pressed his nose against a gap in the huge wooden gates. His nose was very nearly bitten off as a ferocious guard dog hurled himself at the gate. How on earth was Mr Bean going to get his ship-in-a-bottle back now? Slowly, a highly suspect plan began to form in his highly suspect brain.

Late that night, Mr Bean's Mini pulled up outside the dairy. He parked neatly, or rather, he would have parked neatly had it not been for the ladder strapped to the roof of the Mini. The tell-tale tinkle of breaking glass betrayed the contact between the ladder and the rear

window of a little blue three-wheeled car. Mr Bean heard nothing. Maybe it was the black balaclava pulled down over his ears, or maybe it was because he was far too absorbed in Stage One of his plan.

He placed the ladder against the wall of the dairy compound and climbed to the top.

As if by magic, the ladder swung like a see-saw as he climbed up past the top of the wall and lowered him down into the courtyard. Success! Stage One complete!

The guard dog announced his presence with a vicious 'I don't think I like you' growl. Mr Bean knew just how to keep him quiet. He smiled politely. The dog growled his 'I'm going to chomp your leg off' growl. Then Mr Bean produced from his rucksack a juicy bone. The dog gave one final 'Forget it, mate, I'm going to swallow you whole' growl and pounced, jaws gaping. That was his big mistake. The bone in Mr Bean's outstretched arm wedged in the dog's mouth, jamming it open. Mr Bean gave him a pat and headed for the dairy building. Stage Two complete!

Climbing in through an open upstairs window, Mr Bean extended his collapsible fishing rod, looped a length of fishing line over a beam, stuck the hook through the belt of his trousers and unwound the line to lower himself gently to the floor of the dairy. He'd seen this done in a film once, although he was certainly better looking, and taller, than that ugly little bloke in the film. Stage Three complete!

Mr Bean found himself in the dairy's bottling plant. Bottles stood on a conveyor belt that ran all around the massive building, taking them to the machine that washed them, the machine that dried them and the machine that filled them with milk and stamped on the fresh bottle tops. There were thousands of bottles. How on earth was he going to find his?

Then he spotted a control panel. Of course! All he had to do was start up the machine, wait for his ship-in-a-bottle to come past on the conveyor and grab it. He hung his rucksack on a handy lever and tried to decide which button would start the conveyor. The green button seemed like a good guess. He pressed it, and the conveyor belt started immediately. Mr Bean set his torch down on a box. It shone through the bottles as they trundled past on the conveyor, casting a shadow on the wall. When his bottle came past, he would see the shadow of his ship and stop the machine.

Bottle after bottle rattled past. Suddenly, the shadow of the ship appeared on the wall. Mr Bean leapt to the control panel. Which button switched it off? He stuck his torch in his rucksack to give him another button-pressing hand. The extra weight of the torch in the bag proved too much for the lever and it slid slowly downwards. Unfortunately, this was the lever that controlled the speed of the conveyor. As the lever dropped, the conveyor belt sped up and the washing, drying and filling machines sprang into life.

Mr Bean saw his beloved ship-in-a-bottle heading for the bottle washing machine and leapt on the conveyor to save it. He just had time to tuck it safely inside his jacket before he was dragged inside the machine. There was a SQUIRT! SPLOSH! and SQUISH! and Mr Bean emerged from the other side of the machine as clean and shiny as any of the bottles that had gone before him. Hardly had he shaken the soapsuds from his ears when he found himself in the drying machine. There was a WHIRR! WHEEE! and WHUM! and Mr Bean came out completely dry, if a little windswept. Last of all came the filling machine. Mr Bean struggled to escape from the conveyor, but it was no good. There was a SLOOSH! SLAM! and OOOOOYAH!

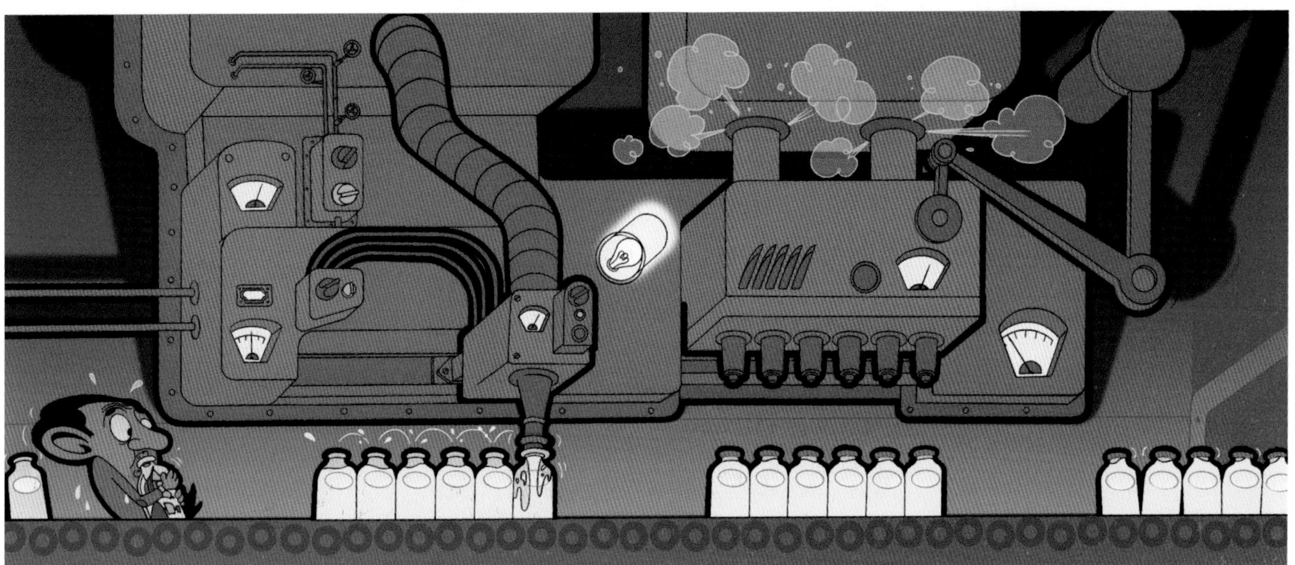

As Mr Bean was suddenly transferred to an overhead conveyor and whisked out to the loading area, a security guard wandered by. Seeing that the machine had somehow been switched on, he decided to investigate. Out in the deserted loading bay, he flashed his torch around. Nothing. But what was that hanging from the overhead rack? He shone his torch towards the roof and picked out a pale, ghostly figure staring back at him and moaning a most terrifyingly pale, ghostly moan. With a short gasp, the security guard fainted.

The pale, ghostly figure spat a bottle top from its mouth followed by a gush of fresh milk and grinned as it held out a completely unscathed ship-in-a-bottle. Mr Bean was overjoyed. Stage Four complete!

Before you could say 'Two pints of semi-skimmed pasteurized' ten times quickly, Mr Bean was in the Mini on his way home. Back in his flat, the first thing he did was to bend a wire coat hanger to make a special ship-in-a-bottle holder and bang a big nail into the wall near the door to hang it on. The banging woke Mrs Wicket downstairs.

Mr Bean was standing back to admire his ship-in-a-bottle when Mrs Wicket wrenched open the door and yelled at him to 'Stop all

that banging!' She slammed the door so hard on the way out that the ship-in-a-bottle leapt off the wall and smashed on the floor. Mr Bean gasped in horror. The bottle was broken beyond repair and the poor ship had snapped in two!

He picked up the broken pieces of the ship and put them on the table. It was ruined. His wonderful, beautiful ship was now no use whatsoever. Then he spotted the goldfish. the little fish seemed rather excited. In fact, if goldfish could smile with delight, this one was most definitely doing just that. Mr Bean held the broken pieces of his ship close to the goldfish bowl and the goldfish zoomed round and round in circles. To the goldfish, the broken ship was the most exciting thing it had ever seen!

Mr Bean carefully placed the two halves of the ship in the goldfish bowl. The goldfish looked as happy as a puppy with two tails. His bowl had been boring. Now he had his very own shipwreck to swim around! This was the best present he could ever have had!

Mr Bean smiled. Happiness is contagious.

Stage Five complete!

My Ultimate mini

1. Mini Jetcopter

Ideal for avoiding traffic jams and foreign travel.

Twin jet thrusters and helicopter rotor blades to fly up out of traffic jams and accelerate to Speed Of Light x 2.

Extra lights to help see in case it's really dark beyond Speed Of Light.

2. Mini Animal Defence System

Protects Mini from creatures of all shapes and sizes.

Roof defences protect against hostile pigeons lurking above parking space.

Bug swatter windscreen wipers eliminate insects before they hit the windscreen.

Poop scoop senses piles of poop and scoops them away, avoiding nasty splatters.

Cat bumper humanely catches suicidal cats that leap out into the road.

Roof sensor detects approaching dogs and activates electric dog deterrent.

3. Cross Country Off Roader

Just what you need for a quiet day out in the country.

High-level driving position allows good visibility over hedges, cows, farmers, etc.

Picnic platform provides pleasant place to eat away from mud and horrid cow pats.

Blackberry collection device avoids scratching hands on prickly bushes.

Path clearing tool cuts through hedges, fences, forests, cottages, etc.

Caterpillar tracks will cross grass, mud, marsh, quicksand, gardens or allotments.

4. Coastal Cruiser

Find a quiet beach away from the crowds.

Periscope for use at depths of up to 500 metres to spot nice beaches on shore.

Fins for greater underwater stability.

Supercharged windscreen wipers for underwater visibility.

Anti-swimmer prod to keep nosey bathers away.

Sonar to warn of approaching whales, oil tankers, etc.

Torpedo to deal with approaching whales, oil tankers, etc.

Mega spear gun to ward of great white sharks, giant squids, man-eating haddocks.

Oxygen supply lasts up to three days.

Propellor for forward propulsion up to 25 knots.

WHAT'S IN THE BOOT?

an you find the following ings in the Mini's boot? ne words can read rwards, backwards, down or diagonally.

HOES, TEDDY, WRENCH, ENNIS BALL, FISH, AMMER, SPADE, JACK, HEEL, KEYS.

L E E H W S H O E S W Y
K T D W F Q P U J T R A
T E N N I S B A L L E N
P D Y W S B C S D M N D
J D M S H K E Y S E C L
K Y A P K R E M M A H K

Mr Bean has cunningly hidden a number of words in this grid of letters. They are all things that he could see as he looked around his room. They can read forwards, backwards, diagonally, up or down. The words you are looking for are:

PILLOW, WARDROBE, FISHBOWL, CHEST, BED, CURTAINS, CARPET, LAMP, WINDOW, TELLY, DOORKNOB and **CHAIR.**

See if you can find them all.

D O O R K N O B F M
T E P R A C H E S T
C N B S T E C P F D
U B R O F B H D W T
R C T I R Q A X O S
T E L L Y D I U D E
A W K A D K R L N H
I I P M C A P A I J
N N O P I L L O W I
S W L W O B H S I F

HOLIDAY HAVOC

Mr Bean has been rushing around all morning getting ready to go on holiday. Unfortunately, he was in such a hurry that when he wrote down his list of important things not to forget, he got the letters of each word all jumbled up!

Can you help him decipher his list to make sure that he doesn't leave anything behind?

SPARSTOP

SLUGSENSAS

TANUSH

YOMEN

WANDICHESS

TOSHRS

YEDTD

DANLASS

KSSCO

TEVS

AMPSYAJ

RATUNPENDS

SPRING CLEAN

Mr Bean was woken from a deep sleep by a strange twittering sound. If it hadn't been for the strange twittering sound, he was sure he could have slept for days, maybe even a week, maybe even a year, maybe he would have woken up with a great long beard and covered in cobwebs . . . What was that annoying twittering?

The two little birds which had been twittering happily on the window ledge flew off when Mr Bean peered out. It seemed very Spring-like outside. Of course! It seemed Spring-like because it was Spring!

Mr Bean checked his calendar. It was time for Spring cleaning, and by the look of his appallingly untidy, grimy flat, Spring hadn't come a moment too soon.

Still wearing his pyjamas, Mr Bean rushed to the kitchen and filled his mop bucket with water. He tutted when the head of his mop fell off.

What he needed now was one of his stunningly clever ideas. Then it came to him. Teddy could save the day. He would make an ideal substitute mop head. It was brave of Teddy to volunteer. He was even more heroic when Mr Bean needed something to wipe around the toilet bowl . . .

Having made a start, Mr Bean decided to wash his clothes, his bed linen, his towels, his curtains and everything else that he could fit into the washing machine, including Teddy. Last thing to go in were his pyjamas, leaving nothing for Mr Bean to wear except an old cardboard box. It felt quite comfy. Mr Bean couldn't understand why more people didn't wear cardboard boxes. When he got stuck in the doorway on his way to hang out the washing, he thought that was probably one reason why cardboard boxes had never quite been the height of fashion.

Replacing the cardboard box with a couple of adapted bin liners, Mr Bean set about dusting, polishing and vacuum cleaning the entire flat. Teddy had dried off enough to help and rode on the vacuum cleaner as a fresh and bright Spring-cleaning mascot. He caused a bit of a panic when he toppled off and was sucked up inside. He didn't look quite so fresh and bright when Mr Bean dragged him out of the dust bag.

Mr Bean checked his list of things to do. His clothes had been washed. Tick. His flat was beautifully clean and tidy. Tick. Next on the list was a bath for himself. Did he really need it? He gave himself a sniff. Pooh! Yes – he really did need it!

In no time at all he was sinking into a warm, bubbly bath. He rubbed shampoo on his hair and set it into a strange shape like a pointy-headed alien. He burbled at Teddy. Teddy just stared straight ahead. Even making devil's horns and a shark's fin didn't seem to impress Teddy. Mr Bean thought he must still be sulking after the unfortunate vacuum cleaner incident. He toyed with his soap-on-a-rope, flinging it around like a yo-yo to try to cheer up Teddy. The soap shot off across the bathroom. Mr Bean sighed and gave up. It was time to get out anyway.

Hardly had Mr Bean taken two paces when he stood on the soap-on-a-rope and slipped, slid, slithered and skidded out of control into the living room. There was a loud WHUMP! as Mr Bean clattered into the vacuum cleaner. The dust bag burst, showering Mr Bean with stinky, yucky vacuum fluff. There was nothing for it, he would have to have another bath.

Sadly for Mr Bean, when he turned on the bath tap, the water that came out was stone cold. What he needed now was another of his stunningly clever ideas. A noise from upstairs provided the inspiration. It sounded like the young woman who lived in the attic flat was having a shower. With a towel wrapped round his waist, Mr Bean sneaked upstairs to check.

Peering round the young woman's bathroom door, he could see her vague shape in the steamed-up shower cubicle. He could also see lots of lovely hot water from her shower disappearing down the plug hole . . . which connected to the drain . . . which connected to the drainpipe that ran past Mr Bean's bathroom window directly below.

Mr Bean shot back downstairs and moments later had cut the drainpipe and attached a length of rubber hose which ran through his bathroom window straight into his own bath. He slipped into the bath which was filling nicely with beautifully warm water. Unfortunately for Mr Bean, the young woman from upstairs chose that very moment to try out a new hair colour – green. The instructions on the bottle were quite simple, just apply whilst in the shower and rinse through. Now the lovely hot water that was disappearing down the plug hole in her shower was a not-so-lovely shade of bright emerald green!

Mr Bean dipped his head beneath the water in his bath then bobbed back up again. He felt so clean. His skin felt so clean. And it even looked . . . green! ARRGH! That stupid girl upstairs had turned him green!

Just then the sound of the shower upstairs ceased. The girl had finished her shower. Great! Now all Mr Bean had to do was sneak into her shower and wash off all of this green dye. Getting into the flat again was no problem. Getting into the bathroom again was no problem. Figuring out how the shower worked was a bit of a problem but Mr Bean soon got the hang of it, washed off all the green dye and switched off the shower again. Before he could make his escape, however, the young woman walked back into the bathroom!

She looked in the mirror at her green hair. It looked awful. She examined another bottle – pink hair colouring – that would be much better. She reached in to switch on the shower. Mr Bean shrank back against the shower wall. The girl hadn't bothered to look inside the shower and hadn't spotted him . . . yet.

She would go bananas when she found out he was there. Luckily for Mr Bean the shower soon steamed up, making it almost impossible to see anything in the bathroom, except the tiny skylight window.

Just as the young woman stepped back into the shower, Mr Bean slithered out through the skylight. Safe at last. Well, as safe as anyone wearing nothing but a bath towel on the roof of a house could be. Slithering down the drainpipe to climb in through the window of his own bathroom seemed like his only option.

Climbing down a drainpipe is a tricky operation at the best of times but when you're wet, wearing only a bath towel and trying to do it without anyone spotting you, it becomes almost impossible. Add to that the fact that someone has cut the drainpipe halfway down and replaced it with some rubber hose, causing the drainpipe to break away from the wall, and you're really in trouble. And really in trouble is exactly where Mr Bean found himself.

The fall might have been really nasty if Mr Bean hadn't landed in a wheelbarrow full of soft, mulchy, stinky garden compost. Mr Bean emerged from the steaming compost unhurt but totally filthy. He was completely covered in the most disgusting muck he had ever been covered in since that bizarre incident at the local sewage works.

Standing in the disgusting sludge, Mr Bean suddenly realised that he could see in through Mrs Wicket's bathroom window. She had her own water heater to fill her bath and it was bubbling away with lots of heavenly hot water. Mr Bean had to get all this compost off somehow, so he opened the window and climbed into the bathroom. To his joy, when he peeked round the bathroom door, he saw Mrs Wicket putting on her coat, ready to go shopping. Perfect! He could have a lovely bath in her bathroom while she was out and she would never know a thing about it!

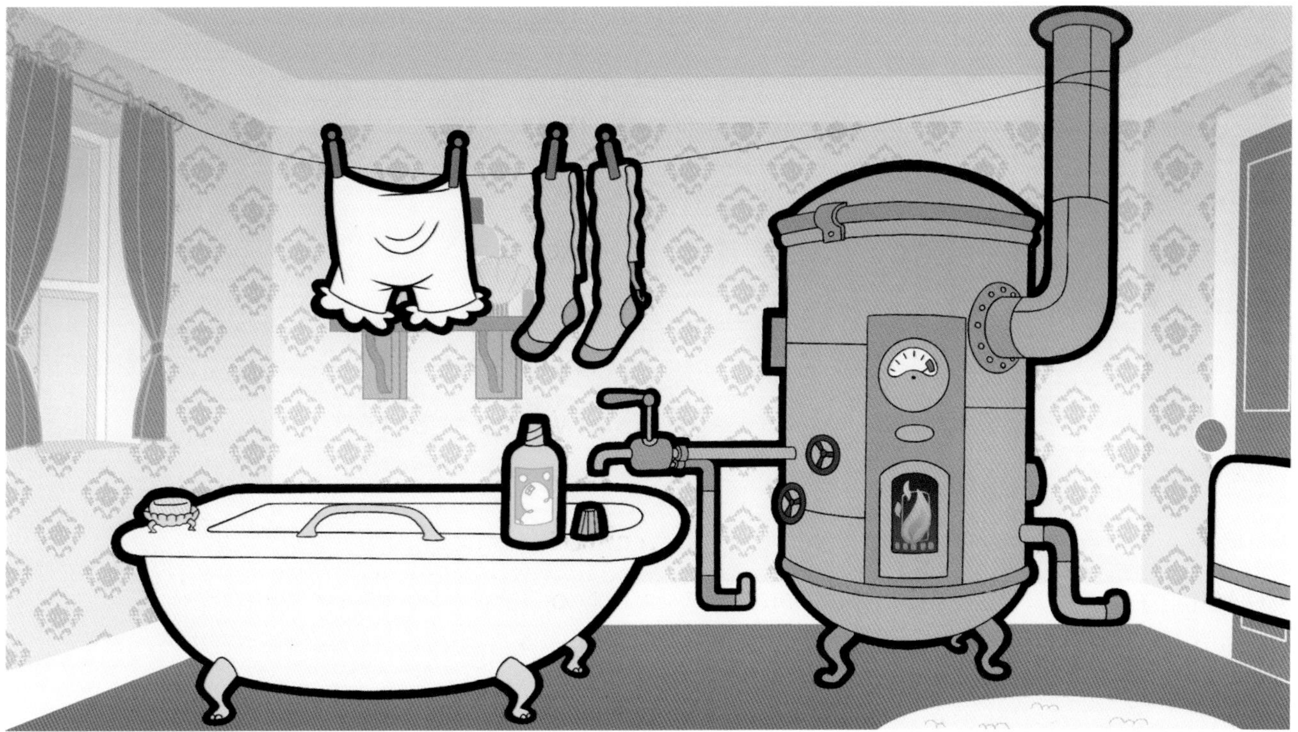

Mr Bean turned the water heater up to its hottest setting, turned on the bath taps and added some of Mrs Wicket's bubble bath. The water bubbled reasonably well, but Mr Bean was sure he could do better. Another of his stunningly clever ideas suddenly occurred to him. Lifting the lid of the water heater, Mr Bean tipped the entire bottle of bubble bath directly into the boiler. Beautiful, bubbly water foamed and frothed from the hot tap. Mr Bean sank into the water.

The heater gurgled and grunted as it warmed the bubbling water inside. Then the gurgling and grunting turned into a clanking and hissing. Mr Bean popped his head up from inside a cloud of bubbles. The water heater didn't sound too good. Then the clanking and hissing turned into a roaring and booming and the lid rattled furiously on top of the heater. Mr Bean struggled to switch off the tap. If he didn't know better he'd have thought that the water heater was about to . . . EXPLODE!!

With a thunderous boom the water heater blew itself to bits in a foaming flood of bubbles. In an instant they had filled the entire room and the door was straining to hold back the torrent. There was a creak and a groan as the door was torn from its hinges and the torrent of foam gushed out into the living room.

Mrs Wicket had had a successful shopping trip. She'd picked up some nice vegetables and was looking forward to making a big pot of soup that would last her all week. It always tasted even better knowing that that fool Bean upstairs couldn't stand the smell of her soup. She fished her door keys out of her handbag and reached for her front door, which looked like it was . . . bulging?

WHOOM! The door suddenly gave way to the tidal wave of soapy suds. Floundering amongst the foam Mrs Wicket could see Scrapper, her beloved cat, and that idiot Bean. This must be his fault! Where was her brolly?

As Mr Bean surged towards Mrs Wicket, he saw her brandishing her umbrella, ready to whack him as soon as he got near. He ducked under the soap suds. He couldn't hold his breath under there forever. How was he going to escape? And even if he did, how was he going to explain all this? What he needed now was another of his stunningly clever ideas . . .

Mr Bean's Photo Album

This day started off badly and then got worse and worse and worse . . .

Mrs Wicket, my landlady. She is not really The Devil, but I think she may be his auntie.

Scrapper is Mrs Wicket's cat. At least, I think he is her cat. She may just be looking after him for her nephew.

Dolphins and seals do wonderful tricks for fish, but Teddy has never got the hang of it.

Impressing Irma in the park.

Irma and her bear, Lottie, came to Teddy's birthday party. None of them were any good at party games.

When I gave the Mini a service, it took a little longer than expected – all night, in fact!

Teddy and I enjoy having a snack and watching telly before bedtime.

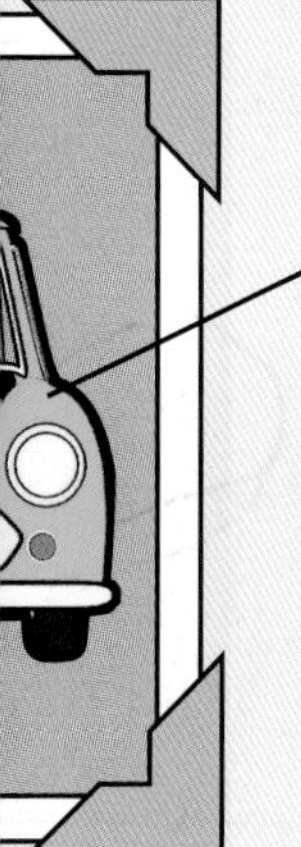

My Mini is the best car in the world, except for when the gear stick came off in my hand on the roundabout outside the supermarket.

It's amazing how much stuff you need nowadays just for a simple day out at the seaside.

SPOT THE DIFFERENCE

The Mr Bean artist has drawn two different versions of the picture below. In the bottom version, some things have been missed out and some things have been cunningly altered. Can you spot all 15 sneaky changes the artist has made to the bottom version?

LATE FOR A DATE

Mr Bean has arranged to meet Irma at the park but is horribly late due to an unfortunate accident with three chocolate biscuits, a skipping rope and the ceiling light which left him trapped under his wardrobe for almost an hour.

Can you help him find the quickest route from home to the park gates?

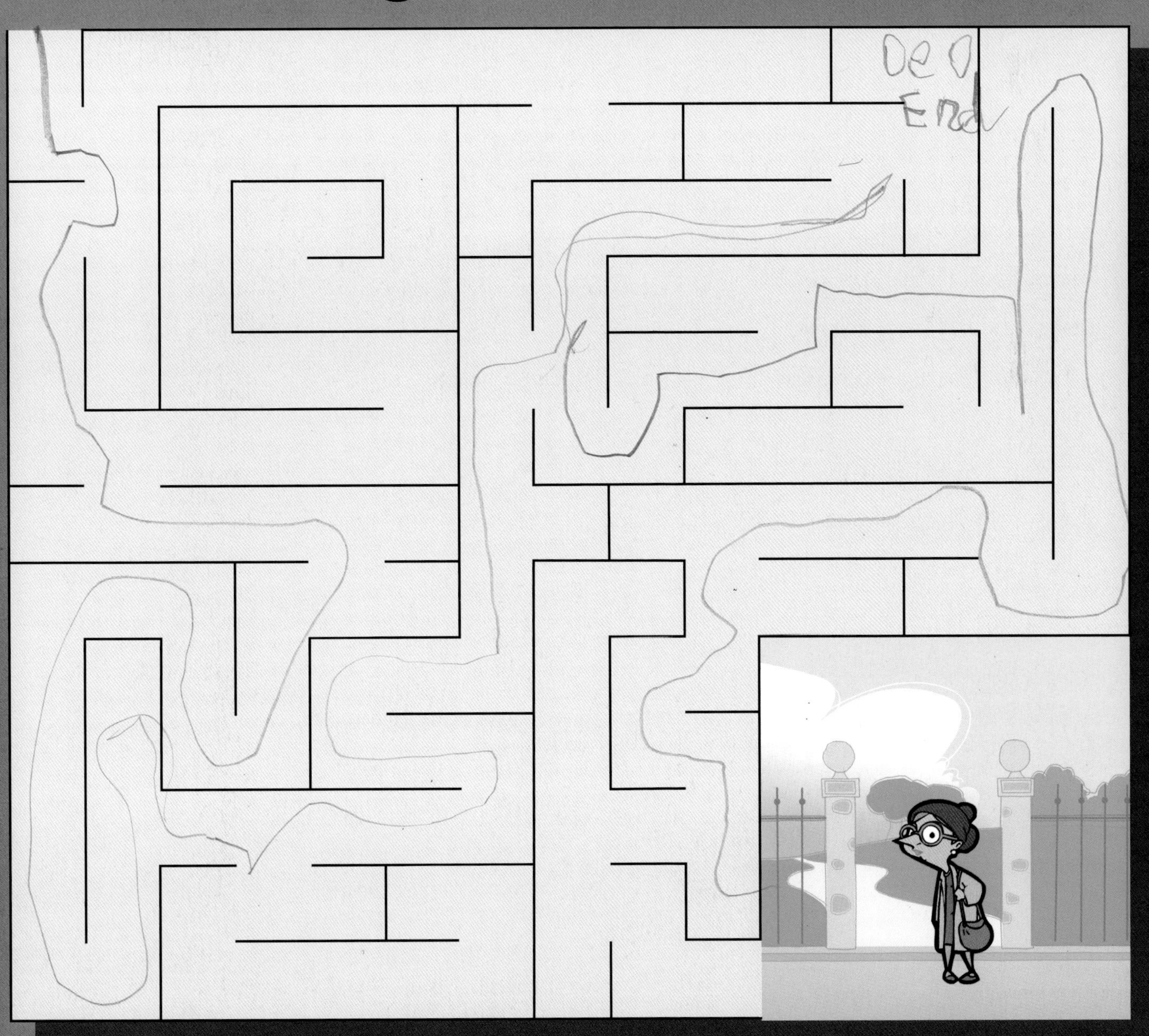

THE FLY

It was a hot night. It was the kind of hot night that makes you feel like you're wearing an anorak over your pyjamas with a hot water bottle in every pocket. Mr Bean couldn't sleep. He pushed Teddy aside, slid out of bed and stumbled across the room. He opened the window and a bit of a breeze blew in with a busy buzz. A buzz? Wait a minute! A breeze doesn't buzz. No . . . it was a fly.

Mr Bean tutted. Pesky fly! The fly buzzed around his head and landed right on the end of his nose. He flicked at it with one hand, swiped at it with the other hand, then blew at it as it tried to land back on his nose. He blew again and the fly swerved towards the open window. Then, with one mighty blow, he blew the fly out of the window, pulled it shut and drew the curtains.

After all that, he was hotter than ever. He lay in bed, kicked off the covers and mopped his brow with Teddy. Teddy didn't seem to mind. It didn't do any good, though. He was still too hot to sleep. He needed to cool down. Now then, where was the coolest place in his flat . . . ? Yes! The fridge!

The light inside the fridge clicked on as Mr Bean opened the door. Cool air flooded out. It was blissful. He rubbed his forehead and neck with an ice cube. That was blissful, too. He tipped the contents of the ice cube tray down the collar of his pyjamas. That wasn't so blissful! That was f-f-f-freezing! Then, as the ice cubes shot out the bottoms of his pyjama legs, an idea came to him.

It took a bit of pushing, pulling, puffing and panting but a few minutes later Mr Bean had moved his bed into the kitchen in front of the open fridge door. Cool at last, Mr Bean happily dozed off. The fly, however, wasn't happy. He didn't like being shut out. He tried to sneak in to Mrs Wicket's flat downstairs, but she threw a cup of tea at him when he landed on her television. No one dares to disturb Mrs Wicket when she's watching wrestling on TV. Champion wrestler Gorgeous Tony Thunderbomb was thrashing Wild Man Willie Mammoth. The fly reckoned Mrs Wicket could have pulverised either of them and buzzed off upstairs again before she could find something else to throw at him.

Mr Bean was sleeping peacefully, cool as a polar bear sitting on an iceberg sipping lemonade with a packet of frozen peas up his jumper. He wasn't sure if it was the buzz-dizz-buzz that woke him or the thump-dump-thump as the fly

bashed himself time and time again against the window pane. Mr Bean flung open the curtains, scowled at the fly and stuck a 'No Flies' notice on the window. When he snatched the curtains shut again, however, he left a tiny chink open. The tiny chink was enough for the fly to peek in and spy another window at the other side of Mr Bean's flat – an open window!

Buzzing with delight, the fly zipped round to the back of the building and in through the window. He spotted Mr Bean sleeping by the fridge and landed right on the end of his nose again. He liked it there. He didn't much like Mr Bean's snoring though. Then one great, snuffling, spluttering, snorting snore sucked the fly straight into Mr Bean's mouth!

Mr Bean sat up with a start and spat out the fly. Yuk! It had been in his mouth! He would have to teach that rotten fly a lesson! Muttering grumpily, he rummaged under the sink and emerged with a can of fly spray. He stuffed it into the waistband of his pyjamas and stalked towards the fly like a mean, merciless gunslinger dressed for beddy-byes. He whipped out his spray, aimed straight at the fly, pressed the button and . . . nothing. The can was empty. Mr Bean hurled the can at the fly then chased it round the room, swiping at it with a rolled up newspaper. The fly buzzed a little giggly buzz and circled the ceiling light. Mr Bean climbed on a chair and carried on swiping, only to shatter the light bulb, overbalance and go crashing to the floor.

Downstairs, Mrs Wicket heard the thud as Mr Bean hit the floor but Gorgeous Tony was being mauled by the Wild Man so, luckily for Mr Bean, she paid no heed.

With the fly still buzzing impudently around his flat, Mr Bean decided to change his tactics. He lay very still on the floor, waited for the fly to settle beside him, then whacked it with his tennis racket. The fly escaped through the strings. He selected a huge book from his book shelf, waited patiently for the fly to settle on the open page, then slammed the book shut. When he opened the book again, however, the fly simply flew away and, spotting a half-eaten doughnut in the fridge, stopped for a quick snack.

Was this a new breed of indestructible superfly? Could nothing bash, smash, squish or squash it? Well, if he couldn't splat it, Mr Bean decided he would have to capture it and formulated a cunning plan. He'd set a trap.

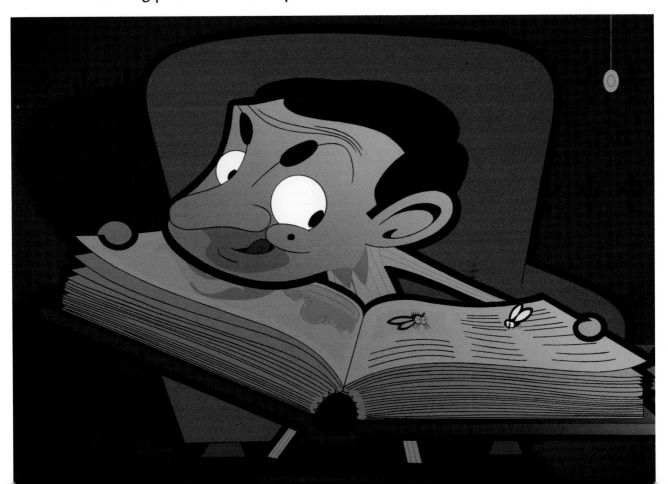

Mr Bean's trap required a dustbin, so he emptied the rather unpleasant pong-whiffy contents of his bin into an even more unpleasant pong-whiffy pile on the carpet. He placed the doughnut on the floor as bait and stood poised to drop the dustbin over it the instant the fly landed. But when the fly buzzed in for a bite of doughnut, Mr Bean wasn't nearly quick enough to trap it. He smashed the dustbin down over the doughnut as quick as he could, but the wily fly was far quicker. It buzzed off along the floor with Mr Bean in hot pursuit, slamming the dustbin down on the floor again and again.

CLANG! CLANG! CLANG!

Downstairs, Mrs Wicket growled dangerously. She didn't want to miss a moment of the wrestling, otherwise she would have marched upstairs straight away and given that idiot Bean a piece of her mind.

Upstairs, Mr Bean revised his plan and set a new trap. This time the dustbin stood upside down on the floor, propped open at an angle with a wooden ruler. Below the finely balanced bin was the doughnut bait. Attached to the ruler was a length of string. At the other end of the string, hiding round the corner of his bed, was Bean The Hunter. As soon as the fly buzzed in to eat the doughnut, Mr Bean tugged on the string, the ruler fell away and the bin dropped, trapping the fly. At last! Hurrah! He'd done it! Mr Bean did a little victory dance and flopped back into bed.

If the buzz-dizz-buzz and thump-dump-thump had been annoying when the fly was outside the flat, the wizz-dizz-wizz and ping-ding-ping of the fly trapped in the bin inside his flat quickly became unbearable for Mr Bean. The solution was obvious – the bin, along with the doughnut and the madly buzzing fly, would have to be flung out the window. The only trouble was, as soon as Mr Bean lifted the bin to fling it, the fly would escape. He needed something flat to slip underneath the bin to keep the fly trapped when he lifted it. The best thing for the job was clearly the metal dustbin lid. All he had to do was flatten it out a bit.

The CLANG!BANG!SLAM! of Mr Bean hammering flat the dustbin lid with a heavy saucepan was too much for Mrs Wicket to ignore, especially now that the wrestling was finished. She heaved herself out of her chair. The chair heaved a sigh of relief. Then she stomped upstairs.

When Mrs Wicket threw open Mr Bean's door, she caught him just as he was about to sling the bin out of the window. She gave Mr Bean such a fright that he dropped the bin. Out rolled the half-eaten doughnut and the fly flew free. Quite what Mr Bean was doing with a dustbin, a chewed-up doughnut and a fly mattered a good deal less to Mrs Wicket than the pong-whiffy pile of garbage in the middle of the floor. She roared at Mr Bean to stop mucking about with the bin. She roared at him to clear up the mess and she roared at him to do it all QUIETLY! Then she stomped out and slammed the door.

Mr Bean began scooping the rubbish back into the bin, scowling at the fly which buzzed merrily around the room. Then the buzzing stopped. The fly had come to rest. But where? Mr Bean stole a glance this way and that and finally spied the fly resting . . . in the fridge. Creeping across the carpet like a commando, he reached for the fridge door and with one flick of his wrist, he whisked it shut. The fly was trapped again! Now all Mr Bean had to do was fling the fridge outside. It was too big to go out the window, so he would have to sneak it quietly downstairs past Mrs Wicket's door.

Sneaking quietly downstairs isn't something that comes naturally to someone as accident prone as Mr Bean. Sneaking quietly downstairs carrying an enormous fridge is even more of a challenge. Nevertheless, Mr Bean managed to ease the fridge downstairs one step at a time.

He had a bit of a wobbly moment when he got caught up in the hall curtains and almost came a cropper on Mrs Wicket's umbrella stand, but he made it to the front door without any major mishaps. Staggering down the front steps, Mr Bean felt a surge of panic as his balance started to go. He teetered to the left, he tottered to the right and then he got his toes in such a tangle that he couldn't tell his tail end from Tipperary. The fridge fell from his grasp and he covered his eyes, bracing himself for the crash as it hit the concrete path. Oh, dear! Mrs Wicket was going to go completely bananas. But there was no crash. Cautiously, Mr Bean peeked out from between his fingers. The fridge had landed safely in a nice, soft bush in the garden.

Mr Bean jumped for joy. He threw open the fridge door and let the fly escape. Yahoo! The stupid fly was gone forever! He cheered, clapped his hands, sang a jolly song and danced around the fridge, whooping with glee.

It was the gleeful whooping that did it. It was the gleeful whooping that woke Mrs Wicket again. Whooping was something she definitely didn't like, and gleeful whooping was something she very definitely hated. Mr Bean froze like a statue when he saw her standing in the front doorway glowering at him. Mrs Wicket could scarcely believe her eyes. What was this imbecile up to now, dancing around a fridge in her front garden in the middle of the night in nothing but his pyjamas!

'Right!' she thundered. 'You're out!' She slammed the door (she was very good at door slamming) and locked it.

For the rest of the night, Mr Bean slept contentedly in the open fridge in the garden, rocking gently on the soft bush and cool at last.

Upstairs in his flat, Teddy had a new companion. Sleeping soundly on the pillow beside him was one exhausted fly.

THE STORY OF THE TEDDY BEAR

Pathetic!

OOOOOH! SCARY!

Teddy bears nowadays come in all sorts of shapes and sizes from tiny fluffy novelty key rings to gigantic life-sized toy bears that growl and roar just like the real thing.

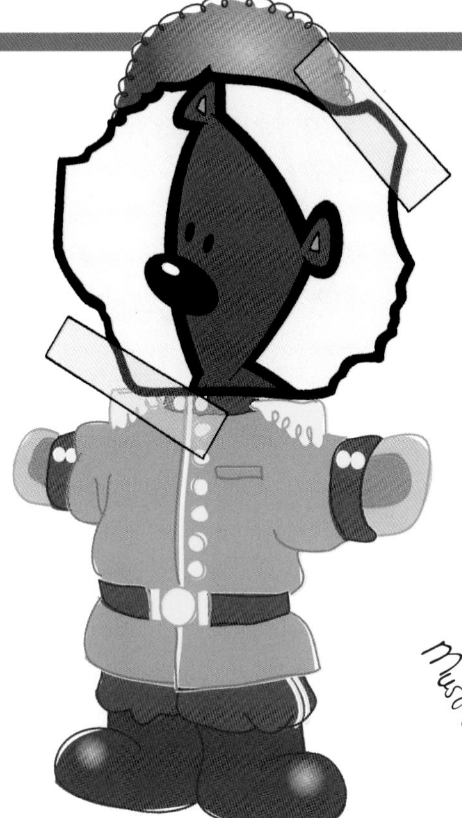

You might think that Teddy bears have been played with by children throughout the ages but they are, in fact, a relatively modern invention.

Contact local Arctophile Society. Question- Does one bear count as a collection?

Quite who it was that first invented the Teddy bear is a matter of some debate amongst Teddy bear collectors (known as arctophiles, from the Greek word 'arktos' meaning 'bear') as the mass production of toy bears started almost at the same time in both America and Germany at the beginning of the 20th century.

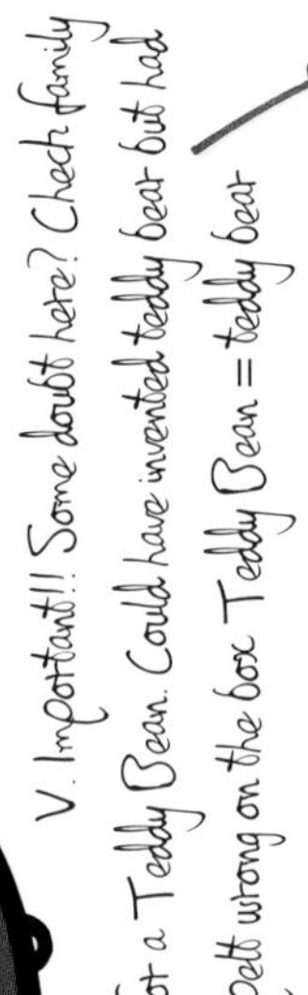

V. Important!! Some doubt here? Check family tree for a Teddy Bean. Could have invented teddy bear but had his name spelt wrong on the box Teddy Bean = teddy bear

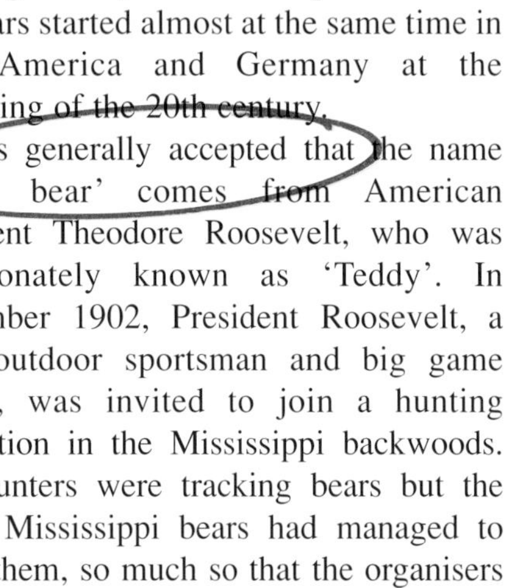

It is generally accepted that the name 'teddy bear' comes from American President Theodore Roosevelt, who was affectionately known as 'Teddy'. In November 1902, President Roosevelt, a keen outdoor sportsman and big game hunter, was invited to join a hunting expedition in the Mississippi backwoods. The hunters were tracking bears but the crafty Mississippi bears had managed to elude them, so much so that the organisers of the hunting party were hugely embarrassed that they hadn't found a single bear for the President to shoot at. Then a young bear cub was captured and presented as a target for the President. Roosevelt was so appalled by the hunters' behaviour that he refused to shoot the little bear and it was allowed to go free.

Nice chap. Must send birthday card.

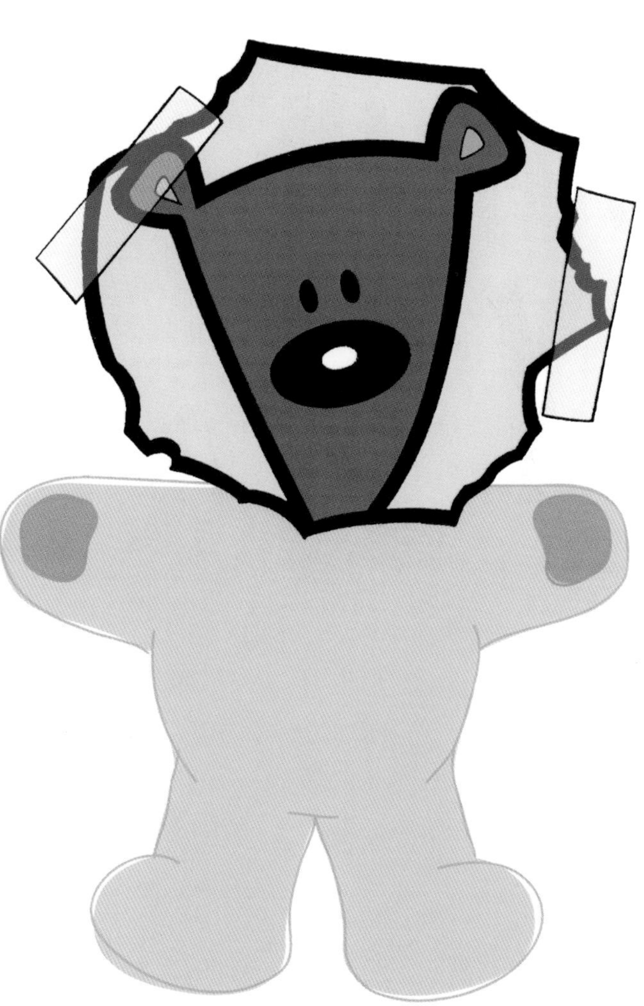

'Teddy' Roosevelt later adopted a bear as his mascot during his political campaigns with bear images appearing on posters, badges, banners and bunting. These became known as 'Teddy's Bears' and the term Teddy bear soon caught on.

Around the same time that the President was out hunting in the woods, two manufacturers were toying with the idea of producing cuddly bears. Husband-and-wife team Morris and Rose Michtom were quick to try to cash in on the popular story of the President's refusal to shoot the bear cub. They marketed a stuffed toy bear and some people believe that Morris even obtained the President's personal permission to call them Teddy's Bears.

Meanwhile, in Germany, the Steiff company were keen to promote their new toy bears. They had been producing soft toy animals, including bears, for many years but up to 1902 their bears had tended to be rather lifelike and somewhat difficult for children to play with. In early 1903, Steiff produced a bear cub toy with movable arms and legs that was far more fun for children. These were loved and cherished then but are equally desirable to arctophiles today. Early Steiff bears in good condition can fetch over £30,000.

*** Take Teddy to next available Antiques Roadshow!!!

Once Teddy bears began to appear in America, people bought them up faster than the toy companies could manufacture them. Steiff bears were exported to America by the thousand and it wasn't long before the rest of the world caught the Teddy bear bug.

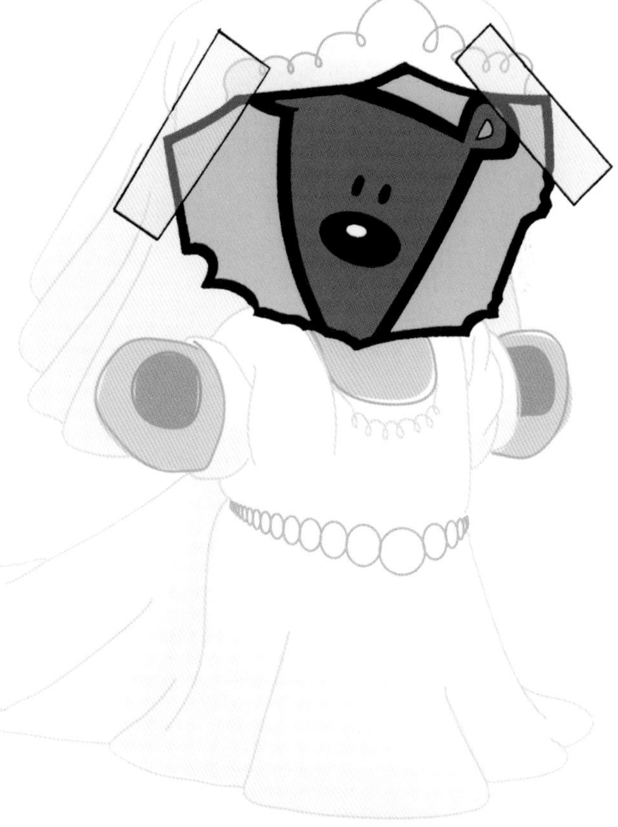

HOW TO DRAW MR BEAN

The Mr Bean artist has been persuaded to reveal some of his secrets and show us the easiest way to draw a picture of Mr Bean.

Follow the step-by-step instructions to create your own image of Mr Bean. The more you practise each stage of the drawing, the easier it will become.

You will need:

PENCIL
ERASER
PEN
COLOURED PENCILS
CRAYONS OR PAINTS

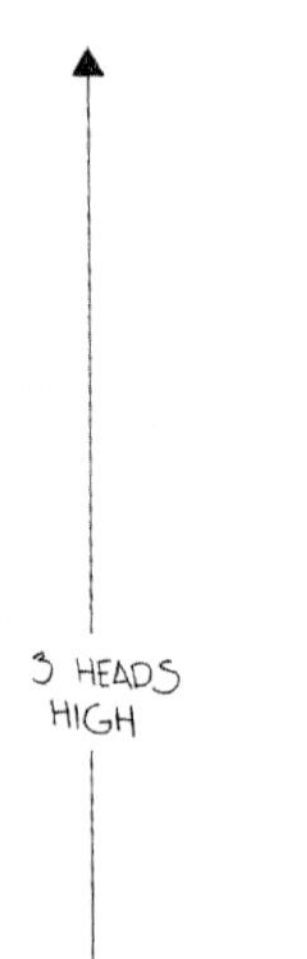

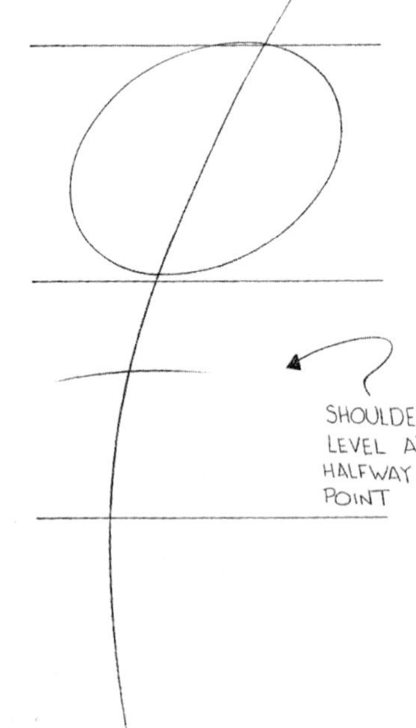

1 Using a soft pencil, start off with a sweeping line. Divide the line into three roughly equal sections. Sketch in a slightly squashed circle for the head and mark the shoulder level.

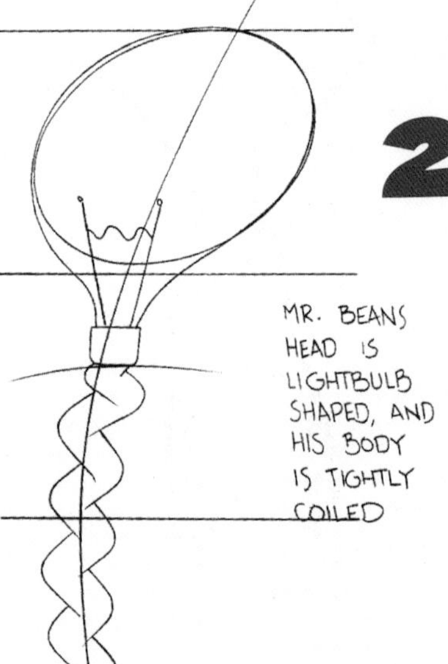

MR. BEANS HEAD IS LIGHTBULB SHAPED, AND HIS BODY IS TIGHTLY COILED

2 Imagine Mr Bean's head as a light bulb and it will help you to create the shape for his neck. Imagine his body as being quite springy, but don't draw it like that!

Sketch the head's centre line and the eyeline to help position the features. A tube at the shoulders and an ellipse at the waist will help to flesh out the body. **3**

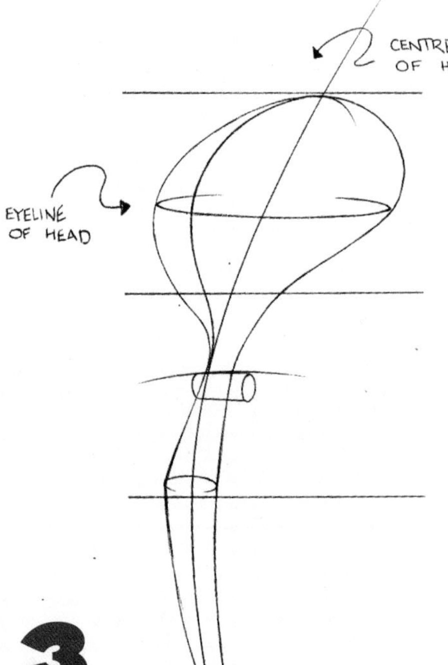

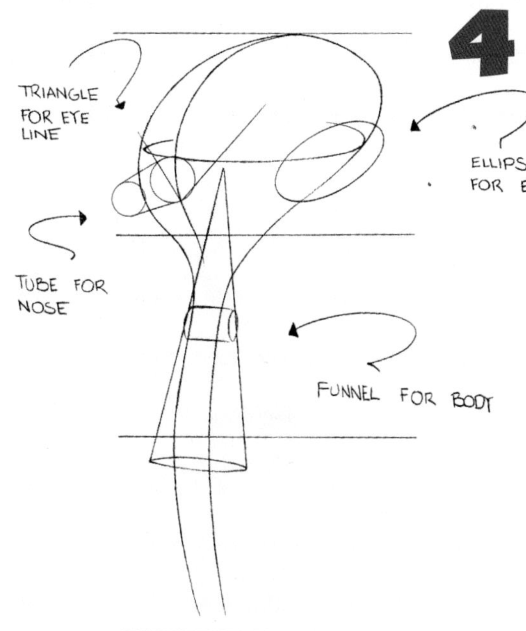

4 Position the chin and brow using a rectangle guide. Add circles for eyes and start sketching the jacket.

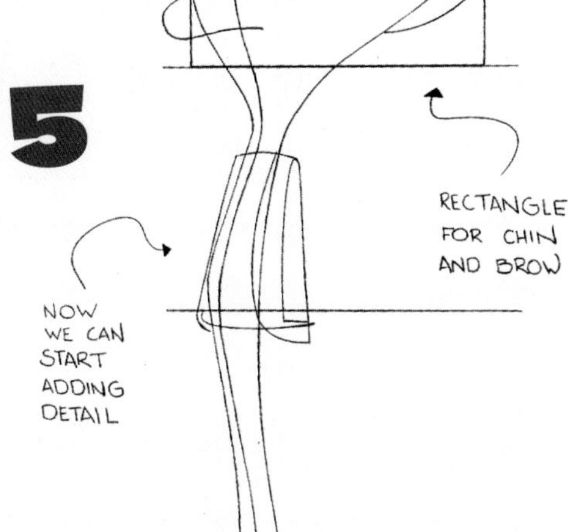

5 A tube will start off the nose. A triangle from the base of the tube will give the eye positions. Use an ellipse as a guide for the ear and a funnel for the body.

6 Alter the construction shapes (tubes, funnels, etc) a little at a time to keep it all in proportion. Rub out and redraw each new shape as you progress.

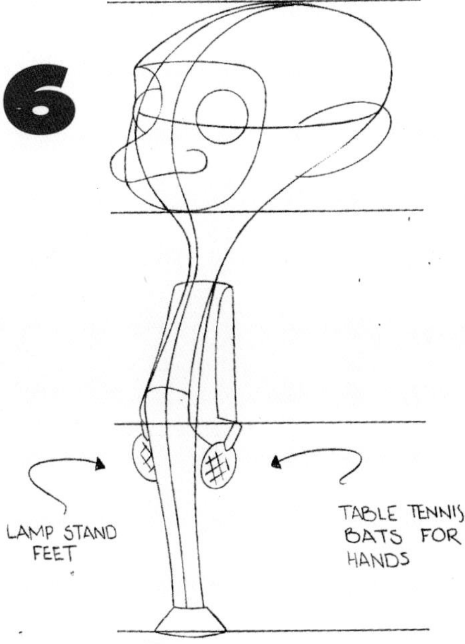

Draw over your finished lines in ink. Rub out any remaining pencil lines and Mr Bean is ready to be coloured or painted.

8

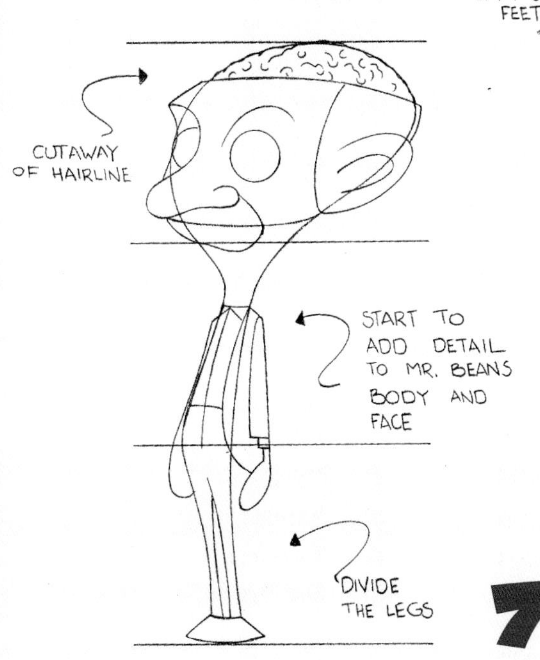

7 Getting the hairline and brow to work properly is tricky but you can do it with practice. Make each change a little at a time until it looks just right.

Mr Bean's

Are you feeling particularly clever today? Think you're a bit of a smarty pants, eh? Then test your general knowledge with Mr Bean's Brain Teasers.

Mr Bean has come up with this list of 20 general knowledge questions for you to answer. Some are more difficult than others and each has a multiple choice selection for the answer.

The correct answers can be found at the end of the book.

Good luck!

1. Bears that sleep through the winter are said to be . . .

a) Completely pooped
b) Stupid – they miss Christmas
c) Lazybones
d) Hibernating

2. Man first landed on the Moon in . . .

a) 1929
b) 1949
c) 1969
d) A cardigan and slippers

3. Manx cats on the Isle of Man have no . . .

a) Brains
b) Tails
c) Friends
d) Ferry tickets

4. When did the first Mini appear?

a) 1959
b) 1859
c) 1979
d) Last Tuesday

5. John Logie Baird invented

a) Cornflakes
b) Beards
c) Vests
d) Television

6. How many lives is a cat supposed to have?

a) None
b) One
c) Nine
d) Too many

7. Loch Ness in Scotland is home to a monster called . . .

a) Lassie
b) Nessie
c) Bessie
d) McWicket

8. Sherlock Holmes' famous assistant was called . . .

a) Doctor Foster
b) Doctor Watson
c) Dr Quack
d) inspector Morse

9. What is the capital of Spain?

a) Flamenco
b) Madrid
c) Barcelona
d) Scunthorpe

Brain Teasers

10. Buccaneers is another word for . . .

a) Hens
b) Pirates
c) Bus drivers
d) Plumbers

11. The Giant Panda bear . . .

a) Eats mainly bamboo shoots and leaves
b) Wears pyjamas all day
c) Practises ballet dancing when no one's looking
d) Hates anyone called Giles

12. What do the letters GB on the back of a car stand for?

a) Good Boy
b) Get Back
c) Going Bye-byes
d) Great Britain

13. What do the letters NL on the back of a car mean?

a) No Luck
b) Naughty Lady
c) Nobody Loves-me
d) Netherlands

14. The legendary King Arthur's sword was . . .

a) Exgalloper
b) Excalibur
c) Hornswoggler
d) A bit sharp, mind your fingers

15. What is a male giraffe called?

a) A stag
b) A bull
c) Lanky knobbly knees
d) George

16. Mrs Wicket's house is called . . .

a) Tarantulas
b) Lilacs
c) Daffodils
d) Wormwood Scrubs

17. Winnie the Pooh lives in which wood?

a) The Enchanted Wood
b) Nottingham Forest
c) The Hundred Acre Wood
d) The Amazonian Rain Forest

18. What is the world's fastest land animal?

a) The cheetah
b) The leopard
c) The greyhound
d) Scrapper with his tail on fire

19. Which pirate in Treasure Island had lost his leg?

a) Careless Pete
b) Long Jim Hawkins
c) Long John Silver
d) Wee Willy One Shoe

20. Which way does the Queen's portrait face on a first class stamp?

a) Right
b) Left
c) Up
d) Backwards with a smile, drinking tea

NO PARKING

Most people wouldn't dream of taking a teddy bear into the bath. Most people would think that a very silly idea. Most people, though, aren't like Mr Bean, and Mr Bean is definitely not like most people. Mr Bean's Teddy is his little furry friend, his best pal, his playmate and, at bathtime, his washcloth. There's nothing like a soggy bear for scrubbing all those awkward places that are always so difficult to reach.

Mr Bean checked that Teddy was paying attention as, out of a bank of bath bubbles, there sailed a model of the great ocean liner Titanic. The real Titanic, Mr Bean knew, was notorious for having struck an iceberg and sunk on its maiden voyage. Mr Bean demonstrated the sinking by plonking his foot down on the model ship. It duly sank beneath the bubbles with a GLUG! and a GLAG! and a GURGLE!

Mr Bean chuckled. He looked up to see if Teddy was impressed. Teddy just stared straight ahead.

He did a lot of that.

Later that day, Mr Bean drove into town with a somewhat damp Teddy strapped safely into the passenger seat and a dripping Titanic leaking soapy water on the floor. Pulling up at the traffic lights outside the cinema, Mr Bean glanced at the film posters on the wall. There was a poster for a cowboy film, one for a

war film and one for a horror film. Mr Bean sighed and shrugged his shoulders. He was about to lose interest when he spotted the perfect film for him and Teddy.

The biggest poster of all was for a film about the Titanic!

Squeaking with excitement, Mr Bean pointed out the poster to Teddy, snatched his model Titanic up from the floor of the Mini and demonstrated its tragic sinking once again. He added a bit of his own glugging, glagging and gurgling for a realistic effect.

As the traffic lights were still on red, he jumped out of the Mini and dashed across to the cinema notice board to check the time of the next showing of the Titanic film. He didn't notice the traffic lights changing or the angry toots and honks from the traffic now stuck behind his abandoned Mini. The next Titanic screening was at 3 pm. He checked his watch. Plenty of time. He skipped back across the road to his car.

The other drivers were complaining angrily, especially the driver of a large, mucky truck. Mr Bean glanced back as the large, mucky truck driver waved his large, mucky fist. Anyone else might have been scared but Mr Bean knew how to stop scary people from looking so scary – you just imagine them wearing nothing but their pants. He imagined the truck driver in huge, saggy, baggy y-fronts and had a little

snigger. He didn't see the traffic lights change back to red. As far as he was concerned, they had always been at red. So why was everyone getting so upset? He snorted and climbed back into the Mini.

Then, a cunning thought occurred to him. He 'd teach all those other drivers a lesson. He waited until the lights changed to green – then he waited some more. Suddenly, just as the lights changed from green to amber, Mr Bean shot off, leaving the large, mucky truck just time enough to trundle forward to the traffic lights before they turned red again. Mr Bean chortled. Now he had to find somewhere to park.

He drove alongside the canal and turned into a garden square where he spotted a parking space. As he prepared to reverse his Mini into the space, his way was blocked by the woman in the car behind. He leant out the window and waved at her to back up. It was then that he realised the entire square was now so blocked with cars that none of them could back up. Mr Bean sighed. He only needed everyone to move back a metre or so. Then a sneaky idea slunk into his head in the sneaky, slinky, slithery sort of way that only the sneakiest of ideas can do.

Slowly, Mr Bean reversed his car until it was touching the front bumper of the car behind. To the horror of the woman in the car, he then shunted her car backwards into the car behind her. Her car then shunted that car backwards. The bumping and shunting carried on until it came to the last car in the queue, a little blue three-wheeled van, which was given such

a shunt that it shot backwards out of the square and across the road towards the canal.

The loud SPLOSH! of the three-wheeler disappearing into the canal distracted Mr Bean just long enough for a young woman to pop her car into the space.

With a frustrated HARRUMPH! Mr Bean set off in search of somewhere else to park. A few streets away, he spotted another space. He was surprised that Teddy hadn't seen it. Teddy had been practising staring straight ahead again. Mr Bean decided to have a word with him about that as soon as he had time. As he looked up, he saw a horribly familiar large, mucky truck reversing into the space! Mr Saggy-Baggy Pants jumped out and laughed at Mr Bean as he swaggered off with the waddling walk of a man who wears extraordinarily large pants.

All was not lost, though. Mr Bean eyed up the gap that old Saggy-Baggy Pants had left between the rear of his truck and a small red car. With a few deft twists of the steering wheel, Mr Bean backed his Mini into the gap, parking it sideways between the truck and the red car. He opened his door and squeezed out, feeling very pleased with himself.

Then an angry voice grunted at him. It was a traffic warden and Mr Bean could tell by the unhappy look on her face that she wasn't at all pleased with his parking. Actually, the unhappy

look suited her face. Some people, he supposed, would be unhappy even if they lost their trousers and found a magic pair with a pocket full of money that never ran out, a pocket full of sweets that never ran out and a lifetime ticket to the Eat As Much As You Like Enchanted Chocolate Grotto tucked in the back. The traffic warden ordered him to move the Mini.

Mr Bean tried to pretend the Mini wasn't his, but the grumpy-faced warden snatched his keys and unlocked the padlock on the Mini's door. Just then, another car drove out of a nearby space. Mr Bean had his Mini in there in a flash. A second later, Miss Grumpy-Face was tapping her pencil on the parking meter. Mr Bean would have to put some money in it.

Unfortunately, the only money he had was a £20 note and the meter would only accept coins. There was a hardware shop across the road, so Mr Bean dashed in to get some change. He would have to buy something, but what? He needed a new screw to fix the inside handle on his toilet door. He didn't want that to come off again. He'd been stuck in there for hours the other day. He'd probably still be there if Mrs Wicket hadn't seen the SOS message he had lowered out the window on a length of loo roll. He selected a single screw and took it to the counter.

To his horror, the shopkeeper behind the counter was Mr Saggy-Baggy Pants! He knew that Mr Bean only wanted change for the parking meter and decided to get his own back for

that traffic lights caper. He popped the screw into a bag and began counting out the change . . . all in pennies. The screw cost only five pence, so the change amounted to 1, 995 pennies. He stacked them on the counter in a huge pile. Mr Bean staggered out of the shop with the mountain of pennies.

Back at the parking meter, however, Mr Bean was no better off. The meter wasn't designed to accept pennies. It was no use. He would have to find another parking space.

To avoid upsetting the mountain of pennies in the passenger seat, Mr Bean drove as gently as he could which, if truth be told, was about as gentle as a hippopotamus in a suit of armour bouncing on a pogo stick. Before long he spotted a parking space. He checked his watch. Good. They still had enough time.

In the blink of an eye, another Mini appeared – a flashy red Mini with white stripes driven by a flashy young man in a green jumper. It zipped into the parking space. Mr Bean slammed on his brakes and the money mountain tumbled onto the floor. The flashy young man trotted into a nearby shop. Mr Bean decided to wait, then spotted a line of traffic cones on the other side of the road. An idea was beginning to come to him and he stepped out of the car to investigate.

The cones marked a dangerously deep hole in the road. Mr Bean borrowed the cones and, as soon as the flashy red Mini was gone, he placed them in front of the parking space. Now

no one could get into the space. Sadly, when he tried, neither could he. He had just got out of his car to re-arrange the cones when the little blue three-wheeled van drew up. It was dripping muddy water from every crack and crevice and festooned with ponging weeds from the canal. Mr Bean waved it aside. It pulled over onto the other side of the road and there was a sickening CRUNCH! as it disappeared into the unmarked hole. Oops!

Blocking all of the traffic, Mr Bean created a special arrangement of traffic cones. The lane of cones that would allow only his Mini to approach the parking space. Once he had finished, Mr Bean drove serenely into his parking space.

Then, grabbing Teddy and his money, he headed off for the cinema as fast as any man who has almost two thousand pennies weighing down his trousers could possibly run.

Mr Bean arrived at the cinema ticket kiosk panting for breath. It was £6.50 for a ticket. Good. That meant he could offload 650 pennies from his pockets. One by one he piled 650 coins on the kiosk counter.

Snatching up his ticket, Mr Bean rushed into the cinema. The remaining loose change jingled in his pockets as he made his way through the darkness to his seat.

Mr Bean at last sat down to watch the Titanic film. The great ocean liner sailed majestically across the screen, struck an iceberg and sank. Then, in huge letters right across the cinema screen appeared the words: THE END.

Mr Bean was devastated. They were so late, they had missed the entire film.

Teddy . . . just stared straight ahead.

MiNi – MONTE CARLO MARVEL

Even older than me!

THE MINI BEGAN ITS LIFE over 40 years ago, causing a sensation when it first appeared in 1959. Although small compared to most other cars of the time, the Mini could carry four adults in comfort with room to spare and plenty of space in the boot for luggage or shopping. Designed by engineering genius Sir Alec Issigonis, the little car was to prove hugely popular, but there were many who had doubts at first.

Surely too many letters i and s in this?

Have a Mini doubt – get a Mini clout!

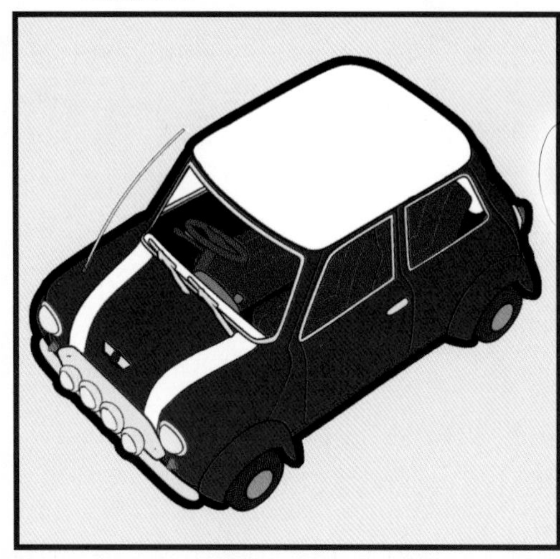

Motoring journalists at the time were very unsure about this strange new car. The engine powered the front wheels, which was quite a new idea at the time. Many of the journalists who road tested the first Minis believed that it wouldn't be able to go round corners properly. They couldn't have been more wrong. The Mini's front wheel drive (now a common feature on modern cars) and superb handling actually made it a huge success not only as a town car but in competition, too.

The fools!

Mine still has a problem at the roundabout at the supermarket

The Mini quickly earned itself a reputation as a giant killer in international motorsport and in 1964 it won the famous Monte Carlo Rally. Those who thought it a bit of a fluke that the cheeky little Mini had managed to win such an important race were shocked and amazed when, the following year, the Mini won at Monte Carlo for the second time.

Hurrah!

Double Hurrah!

The Mini came in first at Monte Carlo yet again in 1966, but some believe that the French motoring authorities could not stand the thought of awarding the trophy to the British car for the third year in a row. After some incredibly complex rule juggling, the Mini was disqualified and first prize went to a French Citroën.

Dirty rotters!

Boo-hiss!

The Mini, however, refused to take this lying down and, in 1967, the British team returned to Monte Carlo, taking first place yet again. This time the victory was beyond dispute and no one could deny the Mini its third outright Monte Carlo title.

That'll teach them!

Triple Hurrah!

JUMBLED KEYS

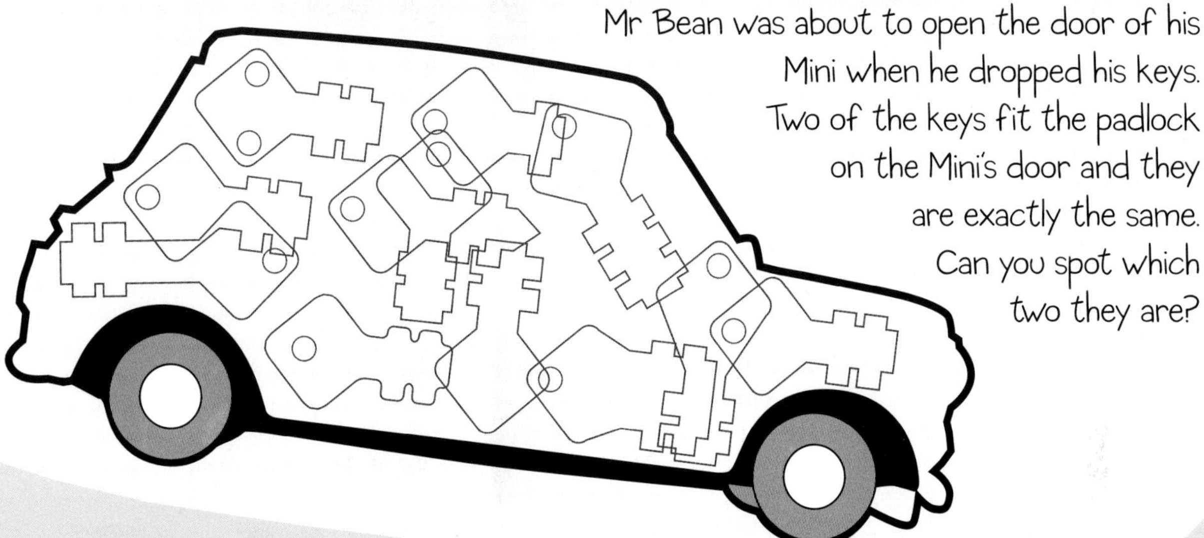

Mr Bean was about to open the door of his Mini when he dropped his keys. Two of the keys fit the padlock on the Mini's door and they are exactly the same. Can you spot which two they are?

In the soup

Mr Bean has bought three tins of soup from the supermarket. One is tomato, one is vegetable and one is chicken.

The tins of soup were a bargain at the discount counter because each of them has been labelled incorrectly.

If all of the tins have the wrong labels, how many does he have to open to work out what is in each one?

DOT TO DOT

Join the dots to complete this picture then finish it off by colouring it in.

IRMA'S CROSSWORD COLUMN

Irma loves crossword puzzles and has devised this one specially for you.

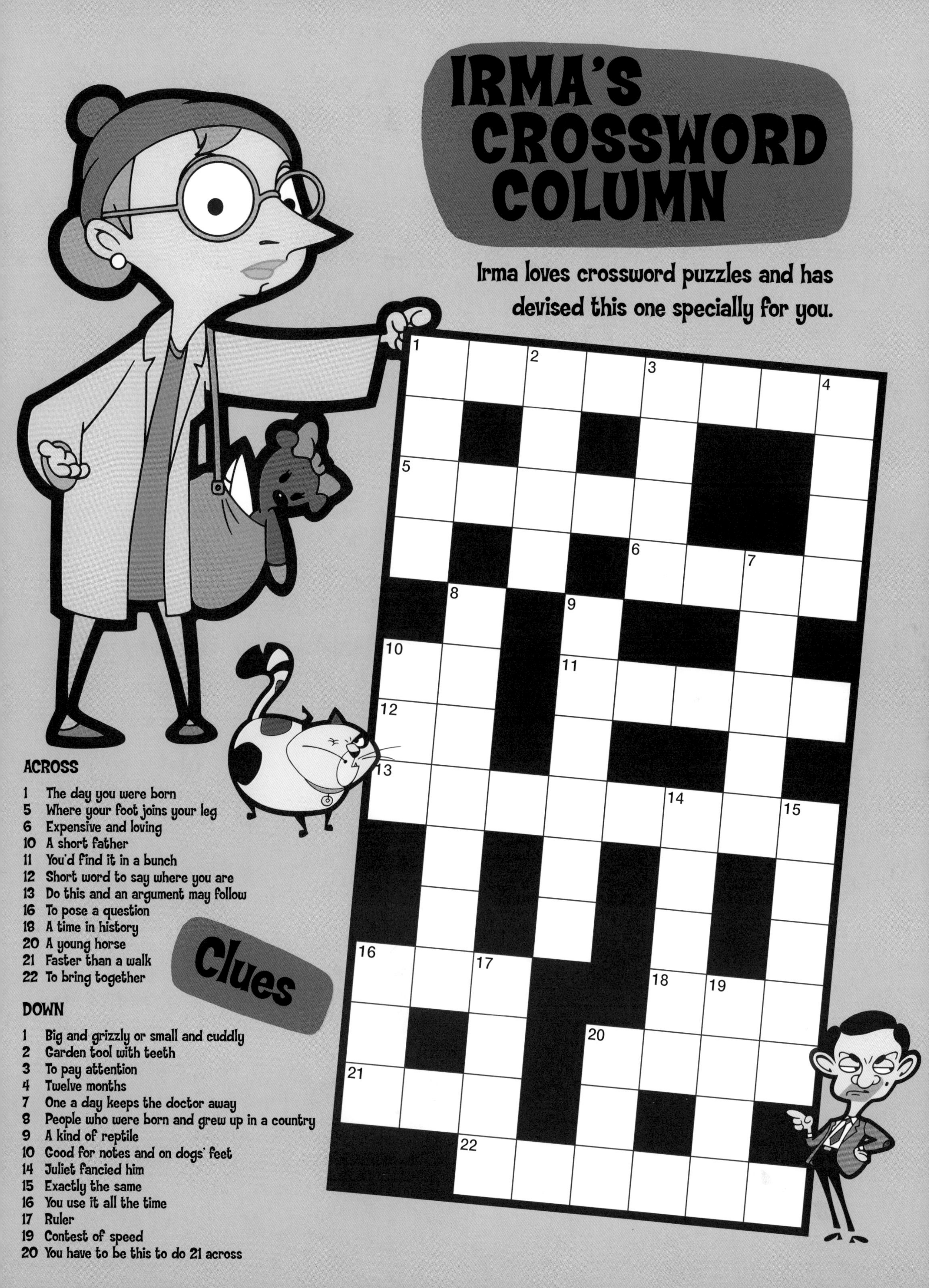

Clues

ACROSS

1 The day you were born
5 Where your foot joins your leg
6 Expensive and loving
10 A short father
11 You'd find it in a bunch
12 Short word to say where you are
13 Do this and an argument may follow
16 To pose a question
18 A time in history
20 A young horse
21 Faster than a walk
22 To bring together

DOWN

1 Big and grizzly or small and cuddly
2 Garden tool with teeth
3 To pay attention
4 Twelve months
7 One a day keeps the doctor away
8 People who were born and grew up in a country
9 A kind of reptile
10 Good for notes and on dogs' feet
14 Juliet fancied him
15 Exactly the same
16 You use it all the time
17 Ruler
19 Contest of speed
20 You have to be this to do 21 across

SIDE STREETS AND BACK ALLEYS

MR BEAN has to get from one side of town to the other as quickly as possible – AND SO DO YOU!

THIS IS A GAME you can play on your own or with a few friends. What you have to do is follow Mr Bean's route across town. Use a coin as a counter to mark your progress.

SPIN YOUR COIN to start the game and call heads or tails as it spins. If you call correctly, you can move forward one square and have another go. Keep spinning and moving on until you make a wrong call. Then, if your final move has left you on a 'special' red star square where there is a message, you have to do what it says.

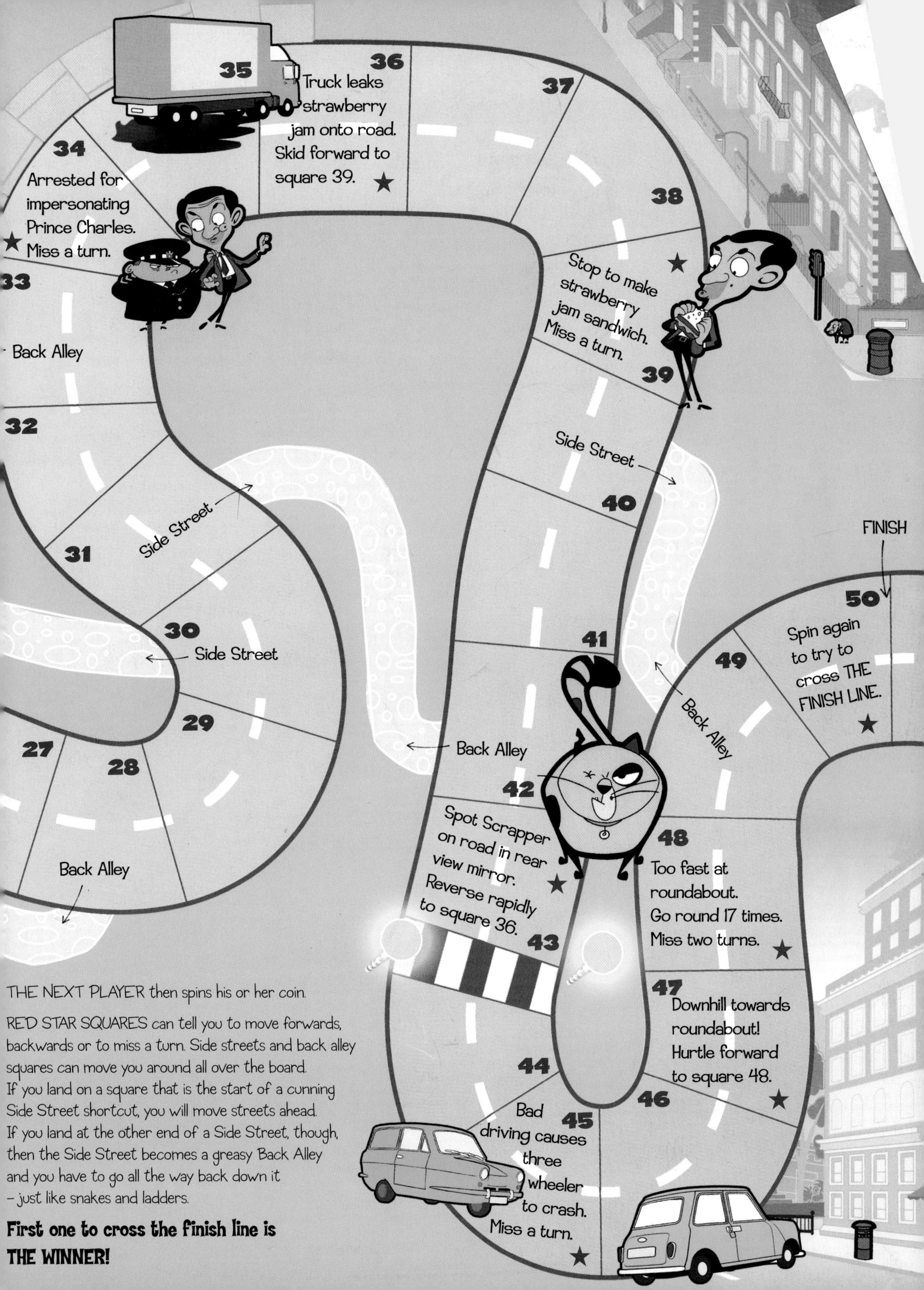

27
28
Back Alley
29
30
Side Street
31
Side Street
32
Back Alley
33
34
Arrested for impersonating Prince Charles. Miss a turn.
35
36
Truck leaks strawberry jam onto road. Skid forward to square 39.
37
38
Stop to make strawberry jam sandwich. Miss a turn.
39
Side Street
40
41
Back Alley
Back Alley
42
Spot Scrapper on road in rear view mirror. Reverse rapidly to square 36.
43
44
45
Bad driving causes three wheeler to crash. Miss a turn.
46
47
Downhill towards roundabout! Hurtle forward to square 48.
48
Too fast at roundabout. Go round 17 times. Miss two turns.
49
50
Spin again to try to cross THE FINISH LINE.
FINISH

THE NEXT PLAYER then spins his or her coin.

RED STAR SQUARES can tell you to move forwards, backwards or to miss a turn. Side streets and back alley squares can move you around all over the board.
If you land on a square that is the start of a cunning Side Street shortcut, you will move streets ahead.
If you land at the other end of a Side Street, though, then the Side Street becomes a greasy Back Alley and you have to go all the way back down it – just like snakes and ladders.

First one to cross the finish line is THE WINNER!

Answers

Page 19

What's in the boot?

Page 20

Mr Bean's hidden words

Page 21

Holiday havoc

1 Passport
2 Sunglasses
3 Sunhat
4 Money
5 Sandwiches
6 Shorts
7 Teddy
8 Sandals
9 Socks
10 Vest
11 Pyjamas
12 Underpants

Page 32

Spot the difference